W9-DEW-502
JUN 0

Stella Batts

Hair Today, Gone Tomorrow

Meet Stella and friends online at www.stellabatts.com

Stella Batts

Hair Today, Gone Tomorrow

Book

Courtney Sheinmel

Illustrated by Jennifer A. Bell

For my godson, Brody, and his big brother, Madden

—Courtney

For my niece Vivian

—Jennifer

Text Copyright © 2012 Courtney Sheinmel
Illustrations Copyright © 2012 Jennifer A. Bell

All rights reserved. No part of this book may be reproduced in any manner without the express written consent of the publisher, except in the case of brief excerpts in critical reviews and articles. All inquiries should be addressed to:

Sleeping Bear Press™

315 East Eisenhower Parkway, Suite 200 • Ann Arbor, MI 48108 • www.sleepingbearpress.com
© 2012 Sleeping Bear Press is an imprint of Gale, a part of Cengage Learning.

Hershey®'s is a registered trademark of The Hershey Company. Swedish Fish® is a registered trademark of Cadbury Adams USA LLC. Disneyland® is a registered trademark of Disney. Junior Mints® and Tootsie Roll® are registered trademarks of Tootsie Roll Industries, LLC. M&Ms® and Skittles® are registered trademarks of Mars, Incorporated. Oreo® is a registered trademark of Kraft Foods. Play-Doh® is a registered trademark of Hasbro.

Printed and bound in the United States.
10 9 8 7 6 5 4 3 2 1

Library of Congress Cataloging-in-Publication Data • Sheinmel, Courtney. • Stella Batts : hair today, gone tomorrow / by Courtney Sheinmel. • p. cm. • Summary: When Stella learns that her best friend Willa is moving away, she makes a wish and tries with a magic potion to keep her in Somers, California. • ISBN 978-1-58536-189-2 (hard cover) – ISBN 978-1-58536-191-5 (pbk.) • [1. Family life–California–Fiction. 2. Best friends–Fiction. 3. Friendship–Fiction. 4. Wishes–Fiction. 5. Hair–Fiction. 6. California–Fiction.] I. Title. II. Title: Hair today, gone tomorrow. • PZ7.S54124St 2012 • [Fic]–dc23 • 2011032121

Table of Contents

Batts

CHAPTER 1

Official Batts Confections Taste-Testers

Hi, it's me again, Stella Batts. I'm writing my second book. It's going to be a sequel. That means it's about what happened after the end of my last book.

I'm going to start with what happened on Friday. I had dinner with my mom, my dad, and my sister Penny. Afterward Penny asked if we were getting a treat for dessert. She'd seen the bag Dad had brought home from Batts Confections—that's our candy store, in case you don't remember.

"Knock knock," I said.

"Who's there?" Mom asked.

"Philip."

"Philip who?"

"Philip my plate with candy," I said. "Get it? Philip, like FILL UP my plate?"

"I get it," Mom said. "Did you make that up?"

"No, Talisa told it to me." Talisa is one of my friends and she's ALWAYS telling knock-knock jokes.

"So are we getting something or not?" Penny asked.

"You are," Dad said. "I brought something home that we're thinking of selling at the store. I need you girls to taste-test it first."

I love taste-testing treats before anyone else gets to try them. It's cool to be first and it's practically like having a grown-up job—Official Batts Confections Taste-Tester. So far Penny and I have been the first ones to test a bunch of things. Here's a list of examples:

1. Sweet-and-sour lipstick
2. Sugar pixie dust
3. Candy Markers

Penny started bouncing up and down in her seat. She's five, so she does things like that. "What is it? What is it?"

"Be careful, Pen," Mom said. "I don't want you to hurt yourself."

Dad got up and came back to the table with a bag—the kind they put your stuff in at Batts Confections when you buy something. It's silver, the same as wrappers on Hershey's Kisses, and along the side it has red writing, like the color of Swedish Fish, which says

"Batts Confections."

Dad sat back down and pulled a little package out of the bag. I knew what it was right away.

"That's gum," I said.

"Good eye, Stel," Dad said. "But it's not just any gum. It's magic gum."

"How do you know it's magic?" I asked.

"It says so on the package," Dad said, holding it up so I could see.

I read the words out loud: "Magical Glow-in-the-Dark Chewing Gum."

"Do you think it can do other things besides glow in the dark?" Penny asked.

"I don't know," Dad said. "You'll have to try it."

"Can I have some?" Penny asked.

"What do you say?" Mom asked.

"*Please* can I have some?"

Dad opened up the package and gave a piece to Penny. "You have to chew it in order to activate it," he said.

"What's activate?" Penny asked.

"It means to make something start working," I told her.

"That's exactly right," Dad said.

Penny popped the gum in her mouth and started chewing.

"Can I have a piece too?" I asked. Then I added, "please," because if I didn't, Mom would remind me to say it anyway.

"Sure thing," Dad said. He pulled another piece out of the package and handed it over to me. Once I started chewing, Dad said, "Okay girls, this is a really important job. I need you to pay special attention and let me know how the gum tastes."

"It's really good," Penny said.

"Yeah, it's minty," I said. "Almost like Junior Mints, except no chocolate."

"I'm going to make a wish and see if it comes true," Penny said. "I wish I was a superhero."

"You can't say your wish out loud," I told her. "Then it definitely won't come true."

"Oh," she said. "Then I'll make another wish." She closed her eyes tight for a couple of seconds. I wondered what she was wishing for, but I knew I couldn't ask her.

I didn't think the gum was really magic. But just in case, I made a wish, too—I wished I could have an aquarium because that's something I've wanted for my whole life. Actually I really want a pet dolphin, but then

I'd need an extra-big aquarium, and I don't think we could fit that in our house.

Penny opened her eyes again. "I'm done. How long do wishes take to come true?"

"I don't know," Mom said. "It depends on what you wished for."

"Is mine glowing yet?" Penny opened her mouth really wide, just like she was at the dentist.

"It just looks like a chewed-up wad of gum," I told her.

"It might not be dark enough in here to see," Dad said. "Why don't you go in another room with a mirror and look with the lights out?"

"Someone has to come with me because I don't want to be in the dark by myself," Penny said.

"I'll go," I said. "We can use the mirror in my room because it's super big." My mirror is the size of my whole closet door.

"Mom and Dad have to come too," Penny said. "And the baby. Do you think if the gum glows bright enough the baby will be able to see?"

Mom is pregnant. Soon we're going to have a little brother, but of course he wouldn't be able to see anything from inside Mom's body, and I told Penny so.

"It can't see us and we can't see it," Penny said. "So how do you know it's a human and not a puppy, or a tiger?"

"I hope it's a human," Mom said.

"But puppies are so cute," Penny said.

"Still, I'd rather have a human baby," Mom said.

"Me too," Dad said. "But right now we have to see about that gum."

Penny spit her gum out in her napkin. "Why did you do that?" I asked. "I thought you wanted to see it glow."

"I want a fresh piece," Penny said. "Come

on, come on."

"Don't worry, we're coming," Dad told her.

We stood in front of my mirror. "This room looks a little messy, Stella," Mom said.

So there were piles on my desk, and some clothes in the corner. "It's not that messy," I said. "Can't we talk about it after we chew the gum?"

Mom nodded. “All right girls,” Dad said, “you each get a piece, and we’ll see exactly how long it takes for the gum to start glowing.”

“Hold on!” Penny cried. “I have to get Belinda!”

Belinda is her favorite stuffed animal. The boy next door named Maverick gave it to Penny for her birthday last year. Belinda’s a duck-billed platypus, but she’s purple instead

of gray-brown like platypuses are in real life.

While Penny went to her room to get Belinda, I pulled down the window shade just to be prepared. When Penny came back, Mom told her to shut the door and turn off the light, so the room would be extra dark. At first it seemed really, really dark, but then I started to get used to it so I could see a little bit, like just the outlines of things. I think that's so weird that my eyes change that way.

Penny and I stood in front of the mirror and popped our fresh pieces of gum in our mouths. Penny said she'd make a new wish with her new gum. I made the same wish, except that I thought maybe the aquarium should be like a pool in the backyard because then it could be big enough for a dolphin.

We chewed with our mouths open so we'd be able to see when the glowing started. All of a sudden I could see this yellow shininess in my mouth. "Dad, look!" I said. "My gum is glowing!"

"Mine too!" Penny said. "Stella and me are like twins!"

"Stella and *I*," Mom corrected.

"And we can't be twins because I'm older," I reminded her.

"But you can't tell in the dark because you can only see the gum so we look like twins. Let's be gum-in-the-dark twins."

"It's still not going to work because I'm taller so my gum is higher up," I said.

"Not that much higher," Penny said.

I'm the shortest kid in my class, and Penny's not the shortest kid in hers. Sometimes I worry she'll catch up with me. I stood on my tiptoes to make it even higher.

"How's it tasting, girls?" Dad asked. "Is

the flavor wearing out?"

"No, it's still good," I said.

"Watch, I can blow a bubble!" Penny said.

I didn't think she'd be able to because bubble-blowing is really hard. I've tried it lots of times with regular gum. But just then there was a glowy circle coming out of Penny's mouth, stretching bigger and bigger.

"Wow, Pen," Mom said. "That looks great."

"That was my wish!" Penny said. "I wanted to blow a great bubble! I'm going to blow another one, even bigger!"

"Are you going to blow a bubble, Stel?" Dad asked.

I pressed my lips together and tried to blow, but all that came out was spit. It was good that it was dark so no one could see. You can see some things in the dark, but not spit because it's too small and also see-through. "This piece isn't good for bubbles," I said.

"Sure it is," Penny said. "You just stretch it around your tongue like this." She stuck out her tongue to show me, and I could see the gum stretched out around it, glowing in the dark. Then she put her tongue back in her mouth and said, "And then blow."

I tried it a few more times, but it didn't work. Then I closed my eyes and made a wish to be able to do it, and I tried again. When I opened my eyes up, I stretched the gum out on my tongue and blew hard. The gum shot out of my mouth and landed on Belinda. The yellow shininess was stuck to her left front foot.

"Oh no!" Penny said, bending down to grab Belinda.

"Let me see her," Mom said, and Penny handed her over.

"I wish Belinda would be okay," Penny said. "Oh no, I wasn't supposed to say that out loud. Now what if she's ruined?"

"It's all right," Mom said. "I got the gum off. I'm going to throw it away."

"Hooray, both of my wishes came true!" Penny said.

All of Penny's wishes kept coming true. Maybe the first piece I got was just broken. "Can I have more gum please?" I asked.

"Actually, I think it's time to wrap up this party," Mom said. "You have to take baths and get ready for bed soon."

"Just one more bubble," Penny said.

"Make it a good one," Dad said.

Penny took such a deep breath that I could hear it, and then she blew her biggest bubble yet. It lit up her whole face until she stuck her finger in it to make it pop.

It's really not good when your little sister can do something you can't even do. If I had another piece of magic gum, I would wish for that never to happen again.

Judy Blume
Tales of a
Fourth
Grade

CHAPTER 2

When the Going Gets Tough...

The rule in our house is we have to take baths every other night, and that night was bath night.

Penny always takes hers first, because she's the youngest—at least until the baby comes, and anyway she'll always be younger than I am. Then when I was taking my bath, Dad started reading to Penny. As soon as I was done, Mom and I went into Penny's room to hear the end of her books. Penny asked

Mom to braid her hair so it would be curly in the morning, and Mom made two French braids. She said she would do my hair too, but I don't like to sleep in braids because it feels too bumpy.

"All right, Penny," Dad said. "Good night, sleep tight, don't let the gummy bears bite." Really you're supposed to say, "Don't let the bed bugs bite," but Dad changed it to be about candy.

After that, I went into my room to read. It used to be that one of my parents would read with me, but now I'm too old for that. I am reading a book that used to be Mom's. It's called *Tales of a Fourth Grade Nothing,* by Judy Blume. The pages are kind of crinkly because the book is so old. Mom says Judy Blume is her favorite writer—besides me, of course!

Mom and Dad came in to say good night

after a half hour. When they left, they turned out the lights and shut the door almost the whole way, but left it open just a little crack, because that's the way I like it.

I don't close my eyes right away. I wait until they're used to the dark and I can see everything around my room. So I waited for a little while, and then my stuff came into focus: my desk with the mug from Disneyland that I use as a pencil holder, the desk chair that

I picked out because it swivels around, the beanbag pillow in the corner that's shaped like a Tootsie Roll, my bookcase with all my books in order from favorite to least favorite, and my dresser with all my clothes inside of it.

My princess mirror and crown were lying on top of my dresser. They came with my princess kit that I got when I was little. Next to the crown was a little rectangle. I knew it wasn't from the princess kit. It was more like a deck of cards, except it was a little too skinny and too long to be a deck of cards. Besides I only have one deck of cards and I knew they were in my desk drawer. Willa had come over on Tuesday, and we played Spit. When we finished, Willa put the cards back in the box and put the box back in my drawer.

What could that rectangle thing be?

Then I remembered that Dad had brought the pack of gum into my room so we could chew it in front of my big mirror. Penny and I had each had two pieces, but I bet there were way more than four pieces in the pack. I wanted to make a wish so bad—that I could do everything Penny could do and even more, because I was older. Probably I'd be able to blow a bubble even bigger and better than Penny's. I just needed to chew a piece of magic gum.

And that's when I decided to do it, right then and there.

I knew I'd already brushed my teeth, but I thought it would be okay. Chewing gum isn't like eating, since you don't swallow anything. Also it's minty, like toothpaste, so it's almost like I'd be brushing my teeth an extra time.

Mom and Dad would probably be upset if they knew, because I was supposed to be asleep. But you can't make yourself fall asleep, it just sort of happens. So it wasn't my fault that I was still awake. Besides, it was just an eensy weensy piece of gum. I wouldn't even tell them about it. Then the next time Penny and I were chewing gum together, I'd surprise them by blowing an extra big, extra fantastic bubble of my own.

I got out of bed as quietly as I could and grabbed the pack of gum as fast as I could. I also grabbed the princess mirror so I'd be able to see, and then ran back to my bed.

I unwrapped a piece, popped it into my mouth, and started chewing. I closed my eyes to make my wish, and clicked my heels together three times, like Dorothy in *The Wizard of Oz,* just to make doubly sure it would come true. Then I opened my eyes again.

It was time to start blowing. I used my tongue to stretch the gum out. Then I pushed it toward the front of my mouth and blew as gently as I could. At first nothing happened. So I blew a little harder, and then a little harder. Then I blew a hole straight through the gum and all that came out of my mouth was air.

Maybe I did the wishing part wrong. Maybe when I wished on the gum and tapped my heels, I canceled the wish out. So I wished again without tapping and I started chewing again. Then I stretched the gum out and blew. But all that happened was I blew a hole just like the last time. I tried two more times and it kept not working.

Willa and I watch this show called *Superstar Sam.* It's our very favorite show. It's

Cecil County Public Library
301 Newark Ave.
Elkton, MD 21921

about this girl Samantha—Sam for short—who's really good at gymnastics, like good enough to go to the Olympics. The other night

there was an episode about her trying to do this twisty leap off the balance beam, and she kept messing up because it was so hard. She wanted to give up, but her coach said, "When the going gets tough, the tough get going." Then she got back up on the balance beam and tried it one more time, and she was perfect.

My mouth was really tired from chewing and blowing, but I decided to try just one more time. After all, sometimes it takes a little while for a wish to work. I stretched the gum out on my tongue again—this time not quite so thin. I moved it up to the inside of my lips and started to blow.

Suddenly the most amazing thing happened: there in the mirror was the eensy weensiest little bubble on the tip of the wad of gum. It wasn't as good as Penny's, but it was there. I blew a little harder and it popped.

I wanted to practice more bubbles but my mouth was super tired. I decided to just take a break for a few minutes, and then try again.

This is
Stella's
room
If you are
not Stella
then Please
KNOCK!

CHAPTER 3

A List of Really Awful Things That Happen When You Wake Up and There's Gum in Your Hair

1. At first you don't even know what happened. Something just feels different.

2. Then you sit up and reach your hand to your cheek, which is the place where it feels the weirdest. And then you find out that the reason it feels so weird is because your hair is stuck there. And the reason that your hair is

stuck there is because you went to sleep with gum in your mouth, and sometime in the middle of the night, the gum fell out of your mouth and landed in your hair.

3. Your little sister comes into your room without knocking—even though she's supposed to knock since there's a sign on your door that says, *This is Stella's Room. If You Are Not Stella Then Please Knock*—and she turns on the lights and says, "What happened to your hair? It's sticking out on the sides, like Pippi Longstocking!"

4. So you go over to the big mirror, and your sister follows you because she's always following you and copying you. Your hair is all bunched up in a clump by the left side of your face.

5. Your sister says, "Hey, that's gum in your hair!" And then she says she'll go wake up your parents so they can help get it out. But you're not supposed to wake your parents up before 8:00 a.m. on weekends, unless it's an emergency.

6. Besides you don't want your parents to know about the gum because then they'll figure out you chewed it after bedtime, which is also not allowed.

7. At first you try and pull the clump out, but it hurts to pull your own hair. Even when you press one hand on top of your head, right by the roots, the way your mom does when she's brushing the knots out of your hair, it still hurts a lot. And anyway, the gum is super stuck.

8. You get your art scissors, because you think maybe you can cut the gum out. It's just there on the side, right by the edge of your bangs. So if you cut it, it will just look like you have a little bit more bangs.

9. Once you have the scissors, you sit down right in front of the mirror and get to work. For an eensy weensy piece of gum, it sure is stuck to a lot of your hair. You make sure to cut so it matches up with the bangs you already have.

10. Then your sister brings over the princess mirror so you can hold it up the way they do at the hair salon and see all the angles. You notice that the bangs on the left side go back on your head a little more than the ones of the right, so you decide to even it out.

11. As you are trimming some more your sister says, "I think you're cutting too much."

12. You look in the mirror and see that she's right: you have way too many bangs. They

go all the way around to right by your ears, and you look so ugly that you wish you could scoop back all the hair on the floor and make it stick back to your head.

13. When you start to cry your sister says, "I'm waking up Mom and Dad. This is definitely an emergency."

CHAPTER 4

The Punishment

When Mom came in the room she said, "Oh, Stella, what did you do?" That's how I knew it was really, really bad, because usually parents pretend that everything is okay. I started crying even more, and then I couldn't even tell her what happened because it was too hard to talk.

Mom rubbed my back, which always helps when I'm sad about something.

"I think the gum jumped in her hair,"

Penny told her. "I'm not going to take my braids out in case it tries to jump in mine."

"You got gum in your hair?" Mom asked. "Why didn't you tell me before you took to it with scissors? I could've gotten it out with peanut butter."

"I didn't know!" I cried. "It was stuck right by the side." I put my hand by my left ear to show her exactly where. "How was I supposed to know to use peanut butter?"

"Or ice works too," Mom said, running her fingers through my hair.

"I didn't know about ice either. I tried to pull it out, but I couldn't do it. I thought I could just cut more bangs and it would look the same."

"How did it get in your hair?" Mom asked.

"I don't know," I told her. "I was chewing it last night, and then my mouth was tired so I was just going to take a little break, and I guess I fell asleep and it fell out of my mouth and landed in my hair."

"But your gum landed on Belinda," Penny said. "I saw it."

"I think your sister took another piece after that," Mom said.

"When?" Penny asked.

"After I went to bed," I admitted.

"But that's not fair," Penny said. "I didn't get to have another piece after I went to bed."

"I think Stella probably wishes she hadn't had another piece either," Mom said.

"I wish I'd never even heard of magic glow-in-the-dark gum," I said. "I hate it so much."

"It's not the gum's fault," Mom said.

"Can you fix my hair?" I asked.

"I think it's best to let a professional do it," she said. "As soon as it's late enough, I'm going to call Kidz Cuts and make an appointment."

"And they'll be able to fix it?"

"They can even it out," Mom said. "It'll look better, but you're going to have to wait for it to grow back like it was before."

"Is Stella going to get punished because she got an extra piece of gum and it wasn't fair?" Penny asked.

"I think she's probably already had punishment enough," Mom told her.

I didn't even feel happy about not getting punished because I hated my hair so much. I wanted to go to Kidz Cuts right away, but Mom said it didn't open until nine o'clock, and then she had to call to make an appointment.

It took forever for it to be the right time. When Mom finally called, the person who answered the phone said our regular haircutter, Joseph, was on vacation. Mom said we'd make an appointment with whoever was available, at the first open slot they had, because it was an emergency. So I got an appointment for ten o'clock with Natalie.

KIDZ
CUTS

CHAPTER 5

Batty, with Alien Hair

I'm starting a new chapter to write what happened next because it's really a lot of stuff.

We went to Kidz Cuts, which is at the same outdoor shopping area as Batts Confections. Mom, Dad, Penny, and I all drove over together. I had a hat on so nobody in the other cars could see my hair.

We parked in the parking lot. Dad took Penny into Batts Confections, and Mom and I went straight to the Kidz Cuts. There was a lady at the counter and Mom told her my name and said we had an appointment with Natalie. "That's Natalie right there," the lady said. "She's with a customer right now, but she'll be finished up in a jiffy."

I looked where she was pointing and I saw a woman cutting a boy's hair. The boy was looking in the mirror and I could see his face in the reflection, and he could see me. He smiled and I wanted to scream. It was Joshua! The meanest boy in my whole school! He doesn't even call me Stella—he calls me Smella, which just shows how mean he is.

The lady at the counter said she would walk me to the back so I could be shampooed and be all ready for Natalie. I pulled on Mom's arm. "I have to tell you something," I said.

"So tell me."

"It's a secret."

"Oh honey, you know it isn't nice to tell secrets around other people," Mom said.

"But it's important," I told her. She bent down and I whispered in her ear, "I can't take off my hat to wash my hair yet."

"How come?" Mom whispered back.

"Because that meanie Joshua is here, and I don't want him to see my hair," I said. "Can we wait for him to leave, and then wash my hair?"

Mom told me it would be okay because we could walk to the back where the sinks are—those special sinks for washing hair that have cutouts where you put your head. Mom said I could keep my hat on until I leaned back into the sink. When they finished washing my hair, it would be wrapped in a towel, and by the time I took my towel off, Joshua would be gone. It was the perfect plan, so that's exactly what we did.

Except when I walked back to Natalie's chair, Joshua was still standing there. Natalie started to take off the towel. "No, don't take it off yet," I told her.

Joshua leaned up against the set of drawers where all the brushes and blow dryers are kept. I wished he would just leave already. I'd even chew another piece of magic chewing gum if it meant he would disappear. Then Mom said, "Joshua, should I take you out front to see if someone is here to pick you up yet?"

"My mom's coming in a little while," Joshua said. "She had errands, so I'm supposed to stay with my cousin."

"Who's your cousin?" I asked.

"Natalie, duh!" Joshua said.

"Okay, let's get started," Natalie said, and

she whipped the towel off my head. At first you couldn't tell there was anything wrong with my hair because it was all wet and twisted up.

But then Natalie started brushing it, and Joshua said, "Whoa, what happened to you?"

"Nothing," I said.

"Did you go batty, Smella Batts?" Joshua asked.

"You want me to even this out, right?" Natalie asked.

"Yes," Mom said. "We had a little accident this morning, and I was afraid to touch it myself."

"I'm going to have to make it pretty short," Natalie said.

"Do what you need to do," Mom said.

"See, something did happen to you," Joshua said. "And now you have alien hair."

"I do not," I said, and I was trying very hard not to cry because the worst thing would be to cry in front of Joshua. Then he would say I was a baby on top of being batty Smella Batts with alien hair.

"Joshua," Mom said, "why don't we call your mother and see if she minds if I take you over to Batts Confections? You can pick out a couple of pieces of candy, and that way your cousin can do her work."

"Yeah!" Joshua said.

Mom called Joshua's mom to get permission, and she said yes. I really didn't want Mom to leave me, but I didn't want Joshua there even more, so I said goodbye to her. "I'll be back in a few minutes," Mom said. "Joshua can hang out with Dad and Penny, and I'll come right back here. Is there anything you want me to bring you?"

"Can I have some fudge, please?"

"Sure thing," Mom said.

"I'll have fudge, too," Joshua said. "And Skittles, and some of those chocolate-covered Oreos."

"Anything for you, Natalie?"

"No thank you," Natalie told her.

They left and Natalie put her hands on my head to straighten it out so she could start cutting my hair. I watched in the mirror. Snip, snip, snip. And off went big clumps of hair.

She seemed to be cutting an awful lot of it, but when I twisted around to check how much was on the floor, Natalie straightened my head again. Mom came back and pulled up a chair so she could sit next to me. "I brought you three different flavors of fudge," she said. "You can have a little bit now if you want, and the rest after lunch."

"No thanks," I said. "I'm not really hungry. I'm afraid I'm going to look like a boy."

"Don't be silly," Mom said. "Girls can have short hair too, and some boys even have long hair."

"I'm a hair expert," Natalie said. "I can tell you for sure that your mom is right."

When Natalie finished cutting, my hair was really short in the front. It got a little longer in the back, but not long enough to put in a ponytail or make into a braid. I tried not to cry because I didn't want to hurt Natalie's feelings, but I didn't even look like the same person anymore. What if I went to school and Willa, Talisa, Arielle, and all the other kids didn't even know I was Stella?

Natalie dried my hair with a blow dryer. It didn't take very long because there wasn't that much of it. Mom paid the lady at the front. She called Dad and he walked over with Penny and Joshua. I put my hat back on before they got there, but you could still tell my hair was really short because there wasn't any sticking out the back.

Joshua walked in the door and said, "You look like a boy now! Smella's a boy! Smella's a boy!"

"Girls can have short hair too," I said. "There's no law or anything."

"There should be," he said. "I can't even tell if you're a boy or a girl anymore." Penny grabbed the bag of candy Joshua was holding.

"Hey, that's mine!" Joshua said.

"You were mean to my sister, so I'm taking your candy back," Penny said.

Mom made Penny give back the candy, and Natalie told Joshua to apologize.

"Sorry, Smella," he said. Natalie elbowed him and he said, "I mean Stella." But that's NOT what he meant. And I knew he didn't mean that he was sorry, either.

Dad told me to take my hat off so he could see what my haircut looked like. "Oh, you're beautiful, darling," he said.

"Yeah, I like it," Penny added.

"Are you going to get your hair cut the same way?" I asked her.

"I don't know," Penny said.

That's how bad my hair was. Penny didn't even want to copy me.

"I'm still keeping my braids in anyway,

because I got more gum and I don't want it to jump in my hair and it's harder for gum to jump into braids," Penny said.

"The gum didn't jump in Stella's hair," Mom said.

"Just in case," Penny said. "You have to be careful with magic gum."

We said goodbye to Natalie. I didn't say goodbye to Joshua because he didn't deserve it, but Mom, Dad, and Penny all did. Dad went back to the candy store because he had more work to do. He said Stuart, who works at the store, would drive him home later. As we walked out to the car, Mom's cell phone rang. She answered and I could tell right away that she was talking to Willa's mom because she said "Hi, Gayle," and that's Willa's mom's name.

Mom turned to me. "Do you want to see

if Willa can come over after lunch today?" she asked. "Maybe that would cheer you up?"

I wasn't afraid for Willa to see my hair because she's the nicest girl in the world, and she's my best friend. "Can I see her before that?" I asked.

We were at the car so Mom unlocked all the doors and Penny and I climbed in while she finished talking to Willa's mom. Then she got in the car herself and said, "Willa's having lunch with her family. But Mrs. Getter said she'd come by after lunch—she has something to talk to me about, and then you and Willa can play."

"Okay," I said.

Mom reminded us to buckle up. Then she turned the key so the car started and we drove home.

7
5
6
4
2
3
1

CHAPTER 6

More Trouble

Mom made us grilled-cheese sandwiches for lunch. Here are some things that are important to know so you can make grilled cheese the right way:

1. Cheddar cheese is the best kind of cheese—way better than American. If you don't have cheddar cheese in the house, you can use Monterey Jack or mozzarella, but never ever use Swiss. It doesn't taste good when it's melted.

2. Don't make the grilled cheese too fancy. For example, don't add tomatoes the way they sometimes do in restaurants, because then it gets too drippy.

3. You should cut the crusts off because the cheese doesn't always melt all the way up to the crust, and bread tastes better when there's cheese on it.

My mom knows all these things about

grilled cheese, so ours came out just right. Then Penny and I each got to have candy for dessert. After we finished, Penny asked if I would play with her in the backyard. I was waiting for Willa, and I told Penny I could be with her until Willa got there.

We were outside for just a couple minutes when we heard Maverick call out, "Hey Stella! Hey Penny!"

Maverick is six-and-a-half years old, which is right in between Penny and me, since she's five and I'm eight. There's a fence that separates his backyard from our backyard, and there's a hole in the middle of the fence that's too small for adults to go through, but kids can fit. Penny yelled back, "Come play with us!" and Maverick came through the hole.

"You cut your hair," he told me.

"Yeah."

"It looks cool."

"I might cut my hair too," Penny said. "And also we have magic gum. Do you want some?"

"Sure," Maverick said. Penny went into the house to get it. She had a whole new pack that Dad gave her when they were at Batts Confections, and she and Maverick each took a piece. I said I didn't want any.

"It glows in the dark," Penny said. "And it does other kinds of magic too."

"Like could I turn you into a toad?" Maverick asked.

"Probably," Penny said. "You have to chew your gum up good and make a wish for it, but you can't say it out loud or it won't come true."

Maverick chewed so hard I could hear his teeth clinking inside his mouth. "Okay, I just made my wish," he said.

Penny squatted down and started jumping. "Ribbit, ribbit," she said.

"You know you're not really a toad," I told her. "That's not even what toads say."

"They do too," she said.

"No," I said. "Frogs say ribbit."

"Actually I think they both speak the same language," Maverick said.

Penny hopped around for a few more minutes, and then she said, "Okay, you can turn me back into a girl now."

"Abracadabra," Maverick said.

Really he should have closed his eyes to make a wish, but since Penny was just pretending, I knew it didn't matter.

"Hooray, now I'm a girl again," Penny said. "Let's play hopscotch."

"We don't have any chalk left," I reminded her. Penny and her friend Zoey and I had played hopscotch last weekend, and the chalk broke because Zoey pressed down on it too hard. Then the pieces were too small, so Mom threw them away. She said the next time she was at the art store, she'd get us some more.

"How about if we draw it with candy crayons," Penny said.

"No, then we'll get ants," I told her.

"What about paint?" Maverick asked. "My dad bought some new paint for the den the other day, and there's a lot left over."

"I don't think my mom will want us to use paint because it doesn't wash off," I said.

"We could do it in my backyard," Maverick said. "It's okay if it doesn't wash off—then we'll always have a hopscotch to play on, and we won't ever need to have chalk."

"That's good, right Stella?" Penny asked.

"Yeah," I said. "But when Willa gets here,

can she come over too?"

"Sure," Maverick said. He went to get the paint and Penny and I went to tell Mom where we were going to be. Then we met back in Maverick's backyard.

The paint came in a big bucket. "I love this kind of blue," I said. "It's just like the color of blue gummy sharks. Are you sure your dad doesn't need it?"

"Yup," Maverick said. "He's finished painting and he's building shelves right now. I'm not supposed to go in the den because it's under construction."

"Where's your mom?" Penny asked.

"She took Skye to play group," he said. Skye is Maverick's little sister.

"We need a paintbrush," I said.

"Oh, I couldn't find it," Maverick said. "That's why I didn't bring it out."

"I'll go get one from our house," Penny said.

But the problem was we only had eensy weensy paintbrushes at our house, like the kind for our watercolor set, and those wouldn't be good for making the hopscotch boxes. "We need something else," I said. And then I had a brilliant idea. "Penny, your braids! They're like big paintbrushes!"

"Oh, goody," she said. "See, it's good I didn't take my braids out!"

She bent down her head and dipped the tips of her braids into the paint. It made it look like her hair was coated in candy. It looked like when we dunk things in chocolate at the chocolate waterfall at Batts Confections. Except instead of chocolate, her braids were dunked in paint.

Maverick and I helped Penny crawl

around and paint the hopscotch board. We had to dip Penny's braids a bunch of times to finish it up. When it was all done, Maverick picked up a rock for us to use. "Who wants to go first?" he asked.

"I do," Penny said. She took the rock from Maverick and tossed it into the first square. As she hopped from square to square I noticed that the blue paint had rubbed off on the back of her shirt, in splotches.

"I'll go next," Maverick said. "We'll go in age order—youngest to oldest."

Penny handed him the rock. I didn't mess up the whole time," she said. "It's probably because Mav turned me into a toad before, so now I'm better at hopping."

Willa came through the fence just when Maverick threw the rock into the second square. "Wow, Stella, your hair is so different," she said. I'd almost completely forgotten all about my hair until she said that. I reached up to touch it. Even though I knew it was short, it was weird to feel it.

"We had to cut it," I said. "I know it's really short."

"It *is* short," Willa said, "but it looks good on you because your hair is straight and shiny."

"Thanks," I said.

"Look, Willa!" Penny said. "We made a

hopscotch board with my hair!"

"Cool," Willa said.

"Mav can jump super long," Penny said.

Willa pulled on my arm. "I have to tell you a secret later," she said.

"Tell me now," I said. Maverick was done with his turn, so I told Penny to go for me. Willa and I went through the fence to my backyard so I could hear her secret. "What is it?" I asked.

"My mom's telling it to your mom right now," Willa said.

"Then it's not really a secret," I said.

"Well, it kind of is, because not a lot of people know yet. Just me, my mom and dad, Spencer and Jackson, and your mom so far.

Oh, and my dad's boss, and I think my grandma and grandpa know too."

"Tell me," I said.

"We're moving to a new house," Willa said.

"Really? Where? I hope it's closer to here." Penny and Zoey are really lucky because they can walk to each other's houses, but Willa and I have to drive.

"It's in Pennsylvania," Willa said.

I pictured the map of the United States that Mrs. Finkel tacked up to the back wall of our classroom. "But that's all the way across the country!" I said. A best friend isn't supposed to move across the country. If I were Penny, I would've stamped my feet and shouted, "It's not fair!"

"I know, but my dad says we have to go for his job," Willa said. "And the house will be bigger, so Spencer and Jackson won't have to share a room. My mom says my room can be whatever color I want it to be."

Mom came out to the backyard right then. "Hey girls," she said.

"Willa's moving," I said. "And not just to another house in Somers. She's moving to Pennsylvania!"

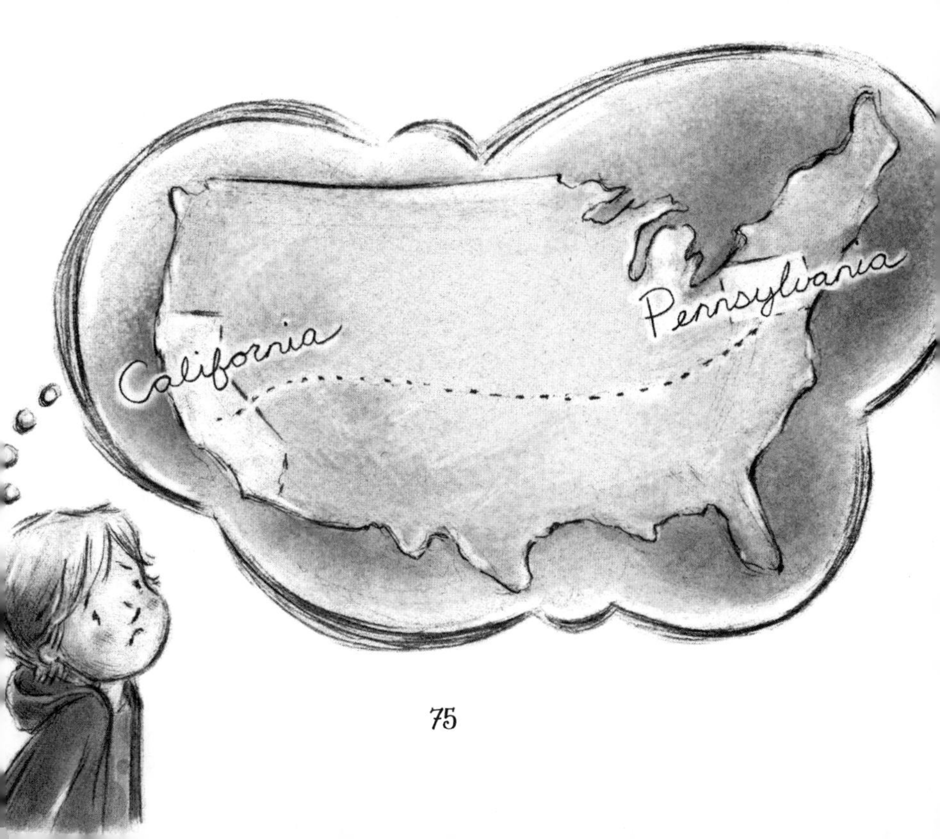

"I know," Mom said. "Willa's mom just told me. We're going to miss you around here, Willa Go-Getter." That's the name Mom and Dad call Willa.

"I'm going to miss you too," Willa said.

"But I think it's all very exciting," Mom said.

"Why are you saying that?" I asked. "I don't think it's exciting at all. I think she should just stay here."

"We can talk about it later," Mom said. "Where's your sister?"

"She's playing hopscotch with Maverick," I said.

"Let me go check on her and then we'll think of something really fun to do," Mom said.

She walked over to the fence and stood on her tiptoes so she could peek over. Even regular grown-ups can't fit through the hole, and since Mom has a baby inside her, she is really too big.

I turned back to Willa. I was going to tell her she didn't have to move after all. Even if her dad got a new job, she could live with us. I wouldn't mind sharing my room with her. Maybe Mom and Dad would even let us get bunk beds.

But before I could say anything, I heard Mom start to scream.

7
5
6
4
2
1

CHAPTER 7

And Then I Really Got Punished

"Stella Rae, what is it with you and hair today?" Mom asked.

Nobody besides me seemed to notice that Mom had made a rhyme: Rae and today. Usually I would say, "Hey, you're a poet and you didn't even know it."

But Mom had used my first AND middle names, which meant she was mad, so she wasn't going to be in the mood for a poem. Also Penny was crying.

We were back in our house again. Mom had screamed so loud that Penny started crying right there in Maverick's backyard. Maverick's dad heard all the commotion (that's a big word that means a whole lot of noise) so he came outside. Then he got mad at Maverick for painting up the cement in the backyard like that, and he yelled. He said Maverick was going to be punished. Mom said it wasn't Maverick's fault that Penny used her braids like paintbrushes, and we would be punished, too.

Penny came back through the hole in the fence, and Mom made all of us—Penny, Willa, and me—go inside with her. She said she was going to wash out Penny's hair and she said I couldn't be out of her sight for the rest of the day.

"How come?" I asked.

"Because I don't want any more disasters today," Mom said.

"But I didn't put paint in my hair," I told her.

"Stella's hair isn't long enough," Penny said, sniffling. "But she said my braids looked just like paintbrushes."

And that's when Mom said, "Stella Rae, what is it with you and hair today?"

"You can wash it out," I said. After all, paint isn't like gum. It doesn't get sticky and make your hair bunch up on the side of your head.

"That's not the point, Stella," Mom said. "Hair is not for painting. And this is house paint. It's much thicker and stronger than watercolors, so it's not going to be so easy to get out."

"How was I supposed to know that?" I

asked.

"Think about it," Mom said. "When it rains on our house, does the paint come off?"

"No," I said. "But I thought it would be different if we used shampoo."

"We've never shampooed the house's hair," Penny said helpfully.

"Am I really going to be punished?" I asked.

"Yes," Mom said.

"What do I have to do?"

"First I'm going to clean your sister's hair," Mom said. "Then we're going to drop Willa back at her house—"

"But Mom," I interrupted. "You can't make Willa go home! I want her to move in with us!"

"What are you talking about?" Mom asked.

"So she doesn't have to go to Pennsylvania," I said.

"I don't think my parents will let me stay here," Willa said. "They already picked out the house and there's a room for me."

"No, of course not," Mom said. "They love you and they'd miss you too much. But you can visit whenever you want. Maybe you can spend a couple weeks here next summer. We'll make sure to plan something really special."

"It won't be the same," I said.

"I know," Mom said. "But Willa's not moving until next month, and right now there's the matter of your sister's hair."

"The paint's mostly dry now," Penny said. She wasn't crying anymore, and she pulled at the end of one of her braids. "It comes off if you pick it." She held out a fleck of paint on her finger to show Mom. It kind of looked like a piece of the shell on an M&M.

"Don't pick it, Pen," Mom said. "I don't want it all over the carpet. Head into the bathroom. I'll meet you there after I call Gayle."

"You don't even care that Willa's moving," I said.

"Of course I do," Mom said. "I told you we would talk about this later." She picked up the phone. I listened to her telling Willa's mom about the paint, and would it be okay if she dropped Willa at home. Then she said, "I don't know how

I'm going to handle three kids, Gayle. The two I have are driving me berserk."

I happen to know that berserk is another word for crazy, and I didn't think it was right at all for Mom to say that.

When she hung up, Mom pulled a chair into the bathroom and set it up by the sink, and the three of us followed her. "Stella and me both got our hair washed two days in a row," Penny said.

"Stella and *I*," Mom corrected. She pulled at the ends of Penny's braids. "Your hair is so stiff from the paint, it's hard to get the bands out."

"They won't be stuck there forever, will they?" Penny asked.

"No," Mom said. She turned on the faucet. Penny had to sit on her knees on the chair so she was high enough to lean back into the sink. Willa handed Mom the bottle of shampoo that we keep on the shelf by the bathtub. Mom poured an extra amount into her hands and soaped up the tips of Penny's braids with the bands still in. Penny leaned back a little bit again, and Mom rinsed her hair out. Blue soapy suds came off into the sink. "It's coming out!" I said.

"A little bit," Mom said. She lifted one of Penny's braids to show me. "But see, there's still a lot of paint left in her hair."

"Can you get the rubber bands out yet?" Penny asked.

"Let me see," Mom said, slipping her finger under one of the bands.

"Ouch," Penny said.

"Sorry," Mom said. "You did a good job with that paint. Let's do another shampoo."

It took one more shampoo for Mom to

get the bands out, and two more after that for her to get all the blue paint out of Penny's hair. She took a towel to dry Penny's hair, and then she brushed it out. Penny's hair is really long, and it hung halfway down her back.

"Oh no," Penny said. "You made it wet so I didn't get to have curly hair today."

"Maybe next time you won't use your hair like a paintbrush," Mom said. "Get ready, girls, because we're going to take Willa home. When we get back here, Stella, you can tackle the mess in your room."

"You should let Willa stay because she's good at cleaning," I said.

"This is your punishment, not Willa's," Mom said.

"I don't mind," Willa said.

"And I'm really sorry," I added.

"I know you are," Mom said.

“I won’t do anything bad with anyone’s hair again.”

“I know that too,” Mom said.

“So please can Willa stay?” I asked.

“Not this time. You and your sister are still punished.”

"Wait," Penny interrupted. "I'm not punished."

"Yes you are," Mom said. "You're going to sort through the toy trunk at the end of your bed."

"That's not fair," Penny said, stamping her feet. "Stella didn't have to get punished when she had gum in her hair!"

I thought Penny was going to start crying

again, but instead she said, "Hey Mom, I just had an idea."

"What?" Mom asked.

"Can I have a piece of magic gum? Please? I left it in the kitchen, but I'll get it right now. Then I'll just wish for my toy trunk to be cleaned. I'll even wish for Stella's room to get neat, and then no one has to be punished."

"I'll have a piece too," I said. "I have a wish to make about Willa."

I knew I said I wished I'd never even heard of the magic gum, but I had a really important wish to make. A way more important wish that anything Penny had ever wished for. After all, what's more important than making sure your best friend doesn't move away?

But Mom said, "No. No one gets any more gum today, or any candy tonight for that matter."

Penny said that wasn't fair, but Mom made us all get in the car and we drove to Willa's house. She honked the horn, and Willa's mom knew to come outside. "Bye Willa Go-Getter," Mom said. "We'll see you soon." But I was too sad to say anything.

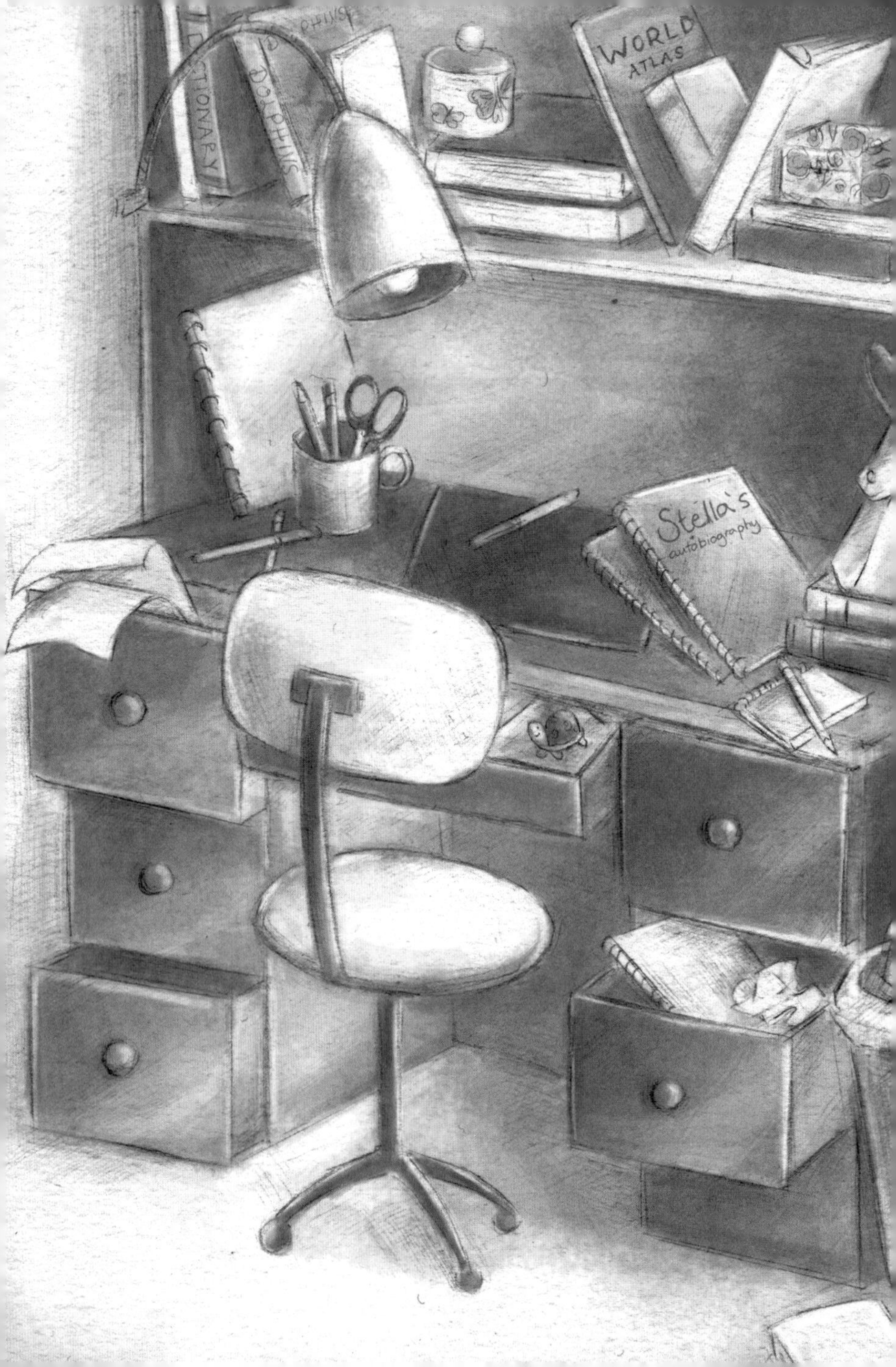
DOLPHINS
WORLD ATLAS
Stella's
autobiography

CHAPTER 8

Missing

In my first book, I made a list of my favorite things. Well, cleaning up is definitely NOT one of my favorite things. It's one of my least favorite things, the same as throwing up and wishes not coming true.

It's hard to keep things neat all the time. Like on my desk, I have my stories, plus pieces of papers with ideas on them for more stories I want to write one day. You can't throw away ideas. What if you forget them later on?

But I knew my punishment was to clean up so I put all the papers together and tried to make the pile look extra neat. When Mom makes a pile, she picks all the papers up together and shuffles them so the edges match up. It's harder to do than it looks.

I have lots of pens too. I started testing out the pens so I could throw away the ones that didn't work. I took a new fresh piece of paper and made a mark on it with every pen. If the pen worked, I saved it. If it didn't work, then I threw it away.

Here's a good trick I know: If you shake a pen really hard, you can sometimes get more ink to come out. So then you can keep it.

At the end, I only had to throw away two markers and one ballpoint pen. Also I decided to save the piece of paper with all the marks on it because it looked kind of like a rainbow.

I put it on the top of the pile with my stories.

There were other things in my desk that I definitely had to keep, like my dad's old gym membership card. It looks like a credit card, which is kind of like money. Mom wouldn't want me to throw money away. I put it in the top drawer, next to my Play-Doh turtle. I have one, and Willa has one. We made them a couple months ago. When we were done, we decided not to smash them up and put the Play-Doh back in the can. Instead, we left the turtles on my desk to dry out and now they're as hard as gobstopper candy.

Willa brought her turtle home. It's sitting on the bookshelf in her room. But soon everything in her room will be packed up and moved to Pennsylvania.

Then I started thinking about Willa again. It made me too sad to do any more cleaning up.

Willa is the nicest girl I ever met. I'm not just saying that because she's my best friend. Everybody says so. Just last week it was Arielle's birthday and she brought cupcakes to school. This boy in our class named Clark dropped his cupcake and Mrs. Finkel made him throw

it away, even though the floor isn't that dirty. There weren't any extra cupcakes left over so he wasn't going to get one, but Willa said she would cut hers in half and share it with Clark. She even let him have the big half.

See, that's how nice Willa is. When she gets to Pennsylvania, everyone in her new school will want to be her best friend. But I won't have one anymore.

I just couldn't believe she was actually going to move away. She's been my best friend since the whole time we've been in school. I'm going to miss her so much! SOOOOOOOOOOOOOO MUCH!!!!!!!!!!!!!!! There aren't enough letters in the whole entire world to show how much I will. Or enough exclamation points.

But I didn't even get to keep thinking about Willa because suddenly I heard Penny screaming. "Somebody help me! Help me!" she cried, and she was just as loud as Mom was when she saw the paint in Penny's hair. Maybe even louder than that.

I got up from my desk really fast and ran down the hall to Penny's room. What if something horrible had happened? What if the ceiling caved in and hit her in the head and there was blood everywhere? I really hate blood, but if my sister needed me to save her, I would do it.

Mom was already in Penny's room. There wasn't any blood, but Penny was crying so hard I figured she had to be hurt somewhere. "What happened?" Mom asked.

Penny also can't talk when she cries. She was saying things, but they just came out sounding like more crying. Mom bent down next to her and rubbed her back a little bit.

Finally I could understand her words. “I can’t find Belinda,” she said. “She’s not anywhere.”

“She’s definitely somewhere,” Mom said.

“She’s not!” Penny cried. “I looked in my whole room.”

“Maybe she’s not in your room,” Mom said.

“But I looked in other places,” Penny said.

"She's not in the den or the kitchen."

"She could be in Stella's room," Mom said.

"Yeah," I said. "You were in my room this morning. I'll go check right now."

I went back down the hall to my room. Belinda wasn't on the floor by the mirror, which is where Penny had been when I was cutting my hair. I also checked on the shelves and my desk and my bed. I looked under my bed, but Belinda wasn't there, either.

"Did you find her yet?" Penny called out.

"No," I called back. Then I walked back to Penny's room. Mom said she and Penny should look for Belinda in the rest of the house. Penny said she did that already, but Mom said they should again anyway.

"We have to retrace our steps," Mom said. "Do you know what that means?"

"We have to go all the places we were

since we last saw Belinda," Penny said.

"Exactly," Mom said.

So we went all over the house and looked for Belinda everywhere. Penny kept yelling, "Belinda, where are you?" even though Belinda can't hear or talk. Mom called Maverick's dad to see if Penny left Belinda over there, even though I knew she hadn't brought Belinda over to Maverick's house. Then she called Batts Confections and Kidz Cuts, but no one had seen a purple duck-billed platypus. She even called Willa to see if Willa had accidentally brought Belinda home, which of course she didn't.

"She'll turn up," Mom said. "Obviously Belinda didn't leave the house by herself."

"I can't clean anymore," Penny said. "I'm too sad."

"Sometimes when you keep things neat,

it's easier to keep track of things," Mom said.

"But I always know where Belinda is," Penny said. "Always, except for today. Maybe something went bad with the magic gum when it fell on her last night, and now she disappeared forever and that's why we can't find her!"

"I promise you that's not what happened," Mom said.

I think Mom forgot to make us finish cleaning because she put a movie on for us to watch. When Dad came home, he checked all the places we did, just in case Belinda was there and we hadn't seen her. But Dad didn't find her either. Later that night we had dinner and read stories. Then Penny had to go to bed without Belinda for the first time in her whole entire life.

SPECIAL
EVENT
TODAY!

CHAPTER 9

Mr. Madden's Magic

I woke up on Sunday and my hair was sticking out all over my head. That never happened when my hair was long. I had to put water on it to make it stay down. I missed my old hair so much.

"This is the worst weekend of my life," I said at breakfast.

"Mine too," Penny said.

Belinda was still missing. Dad said it was going to be Mom's Day Off, which meant she was going to have the whole day to be by herself and do whatever she wanted. "We have a few errands to run and then we're going to the store," Dad said.

"I'm too sad to go on errands," Penny told him. "And I'm too sad for the store."

"I promise you'll get cheered up," Dad said. "Something really special is happening at Batts Confections today."

"What?" Penny asked.

"You'll find out when we get there," Dad told her.

He was probably just saying that because he wanted to distract Penny from thinking about Belinda too much. So when Penny went to get dressed, I whispered to Dad, "What's the special thing that's happening?"

"I told you, it's a surprise," Dad whispered back.

"You should tell me in case I don't want to go," I said.

"Trust me," Dad said, "you're going to want to. Besides, we're giving Mom the day off, and that means we all have to get out of the house."

We headed out to the car a little while later. Our first errand was going to the plant store, because Mom wanted Dad to order some special kind of flowers. Our second errand was to drop off a candy basket that someone had ordered.

After that we got back in the car to drive to Batts Confections. Dad parked in the parking lot and we all got out. Someone shouted, "Stella, over here!"

I looked up, and there was Willa a few car rows over from us. "Hi!" I shouted back.

Dad walked Penny and me over to

Willa's mom's car. He said Willa was going to be spending the day with us. "That's a really good surprise," I said.

"It's not the only one," Dad said.

"Is Zoey coming too?" Penny asked.

"No, Zoey was busy today," Dad said.

"It's not fair!" Penny said.

"You can play with us," Willa offered. Willa is always nice to Penny.

"Bye girls. Have fun," Willa's mom said.

We walked into Batts Confections. The store had just opened but there was already a bunch of people there. Willa, Penny, and I got on line by the chocolate waterfall. Really we could skip the line if we wanted because my parents own the store, but that wouldn't be nice to the other kids. We each took a marshmallow on a stick to dip into the chocolate.

"Just one piece," Dad said. "I don't want you to fill up because you'll be getting a special treat."

"When is the treat?" Penny asked.

"In about fifteen minutes," Dad said.

He and Penny went down to his office, but Willa and I stayed upstairs with Stuart, who was working behind the register. He let Willa and me help out, which is a really fun thing to do. When people give you money,

you get to press buttons on the register, and then it dings and pops open. Then you have to give them the right change and say, "Thanks, and have a nice day!"

A man with a suitcase came up to the counter. "Can I help you?" Stuart asked.

"I'm Eric Madden. I'm looking for David Batts."

David Batts is my dad's name. All his friends call him Dave, so I knew this man was someone who didn't know Dad very well. I wondered if maybe he was visiting from out of town.

Stuart called Dad in his office and Dad came upstairs. He shook the man's hand and told us to wait with Stuart while he and Eric Madden went back to the party room.

"What are they doing?" Penny asked.

"I don't know," I said.

Dad came back a few minutes later. "Who was that?" I asked.

"That was the rest of the surprise," he said. Then he took the microphone that he keeps behind the register and made an announcement that everyone in the store was invited up to the party room for a special show by Mr. Madden the Magician.

Upstairs there was a dark-blue tablecloth on the table. It had little stars all over it that sort of sparkled, and it looked magical. Mr. Madden was wearing a top hat, like the ringmaster at a circus. "I don't like it in here!" Penny cried. "I don't like magic anymore!"

She buried her head in Dad's shirt. A bunch of kids were coming in and sitting down at the table. I saw Maddie Forman come in. I know her because she's in my class at school, but Willa and I aren't good friends with her.

"Come on," Willa said. "Let's get seats."

I wasn't sure I wanted to sit down. Magic wasn't so good to me either. The magic gum got me in so much trouble, and none of my wishes had come true. "Is he doing things with magic gum?" I asked Dad.

"I don't think so," Dad said. "The gum gave me the idea to bring a magician in, but Mr. Madden has all his own tricks."

I decided as long as there was no gum, it would be okay. Willa and I went to sit at the table, and Mr. Madden started his magic show.

First he did this thing with a bunch of cups. He had three cups, and he lifted them up so we saw there was a mini box of chocolate animal crackers under the middle one. Then he tapped the cup and lifted it up again, and the box was gone. He tapped the one on the right and lifted it up, and the box was under that one. He kept going and going, tapping really fast, and lifting up the cups. I watched his hands extra carefully, but I couldn't figure out how he was doing it. At the end, he tapped

all three cups one last time. He lifted up all the cups and the box was gone.

"Where'd it go?" Maddie called out.

"It's right there in your lap," Mr. Madden said.

Maddie reached down and held up the box. "How did it get here? You weren't even near me!"

"It's magic," Mr. Madden said.

Everyone clapped and Mr. Madden took a bow. I glanced over to the back of the room. Dad was still holding Penny, but her face wasn't in his shirt anymore. She was watching everything the magician did.

He pulled out his suitcase. For the first time, I noticed there was a little mesh at the top, like you see on a cage. He opened it up, took out a real live rabbit, and closed it again.

"Allow me to introduce Horse," Mr.

Madden said.

"Horse!" a boy called out. "But that's a bunny rabbit."

Mr. Madden took off his top hat and put the rabbit named Horse inside. Then he pulled a handkerchief out of his sleeve and placed it over the opening of the hat. He waved his wand around, pulled the handkerchief off, and the rabbit was gone!

"What do you think happened to Horse?" Willa whispered.

"I don't know," I whispered back.

Mr. Madden put the handkerchief back on the hat, waved his wand, and when he pulled the handkerchief off again, a chocolate rabbit had appeared. Then he opened the suitcase back up, and Horse was safe inside it.

After that, he walked over to the table and started pulling candies out of people's ears. He made a big pile in the middle. Then Stuart came in with a tray filled with cups of pudding and all sorts of toppings. Mr. Madden said the toppings were magical toppings, and the things he'd pulled out of people's ears were magical too. He said we'd each get a cup of pudding, and we could use the magical ingredients to make our own potions.

Dad brought Penny over and pulled up a chair right by Willa and me. Penny made Dad stand nearby while she made a potion to get Belinda back. Willa said she was going to make something called "healthy pudding." She said whoever ate it wouldn't have any more allergies. "What about you?" Willa asked.

"I can't tell you," I said. "It's magic, which is like a wish, so I want to make sure it comes true."

I clicked my heels three times and made a wish that Willa wouldn't move away. Then I made up a recipe for Magical Get-Your-Best-Friend-to-Not-Move-Away Pudding. This is what you do:

1. Start with one cup of chocolate pudding
2. Add in 14 green M&Ms
3. Then put in jelly beans, gummy worms, and a couple of cookie dough balls
4. Top it off with a pinch of rainbow sprinkles
5. Give it to your best friend to taste, and take a bite yourself

Mr. Madden walked over to us. "What do you think, girls?"

"It's fun," I said.

"That's good to hear," he told us. "I hope to be back next month." He winked at Dad.

"But I won't be here," Willa told him. "I'm moving away."

Mr. Madden reached into his jacket pocket and pulled out a rose. But it wasn't a regular rose, because the flower part was made of chocolate. "Here you are, young lady. Something for you to remember me by."

"Hey magic man!" a boy called from the other end of the table. "I need more red jelly beans!"

"Duty calls," Mr. Madden said. "I'll catch you guys later."

"Do you think we should make a magical display here at the store?" Dad asked when

Mr. Madden walked away. “We’ve had the candy garden for awhile, so it may be time for a change.”

“I don’t know,” I said. “People love the candy waterfall, and we don’t even know if

the magic works yet."

"Think about it," Dad said. "We don't have to decide today."

Dad's cell phone rang a few minutes later. He answered it and then said, "Penny, it's for you."

"Hi, who is this?" she asked when she took the phone. "Oh, hi Mommy. What do you have to tell me?"

I wondered why Mom wanted to talk to Penny and not me.

Then Penny yelled, "She found Belinda! Mom found Belinda!" She handed the phone back to Dad and ran over to Mr. Madden to tell him her potion worked.

When she came back

over, Penny said she was ready to go home because she wanted to see Belinda right away. Willa and I were done with our potions anyway, so we said goodbye to everyone at Batts Confections and headed home.

CHAPTER 10

I Believe in Magic (But Only Sort Of)

Mom found Belinda in one of the kitchen cabinets! Isn't that the craziest place for a stuffed duck-billed platypus?

When Mom told us, Penny remembered what had happened. She brought the gum back into the kitchen after she gave some to Maverick. Belinda was on the kitchen table, and Penny decided to hide her in the cabinet. That way if the gum really was magic jumping gum, Belinda would be totally safe.

"My pudding potion worked!" Penny said, dancing around the room with Belinda. "Belinda is back!"

I wondered if my potion would work. Maybe when Mrs. Getter came to pick up Willa, she'd announce that they decided not to move after all.

Willa and I went to my room to play because her mom wouldn't be there for another half hour. "What do you want to play?" Willa asked.

"How about Spit?" I asked.

Willa said okay, and I got the cards and shuffled them up. Dad can do this cool thing when he shuffles cards, and then bends them like a bridge. It's hard for me to do because my hands are too small. Usually I just spread the cards out and mix them up, and then put them back together again.

Then I dealt the cards. We each got half the deck, and we made our piles like we're supposed to. Willa said, "One, two, three, spit!" and we both turned a card over and started playing.

It's really hard to explain how the game goes, but I'll try. You have to pile cards on top of each other in order, but it doesn't matter if the numbers go up or down. If a 5 card is

showing, you can put a 4 or a 6 on top of it. And you keep going until all your cards are gone.

We're both really good at Spit, which makes the game last longer. You win when you're totally out of cards. I wonder how long the longest game of Spit ever lasted. Sometimes I think maybe Willa and I will get the world record.

That day we played until Penny came in to say Willa's mom had just driven up. Willa was winning, but the game still wasn't over. "I can leave the cards out, and then when you come over again, we can finish," I said.

"But it's kind of messy," Willa said. See what I mean about how neat and clean she is? "We should finish right now."

"Your mom won't mind?" I asked.

Willa shook her head and we went back

to playing. Penny sat on my bed and watched us. My mom and Willa's mom came into my room and Willa's mom said, "Honey, we have to get going."

"I don't want to," Willa said.

"I know, hon," Mrs. Getter said. "But I have to get the boys."

Willa stood up but she didn't go over to her mom. "No," she said. "I don't want to."

"Willa," Mrs. Getter said. "Spencer and Jackson are waiting."

"I don't want to leave!" Willa shouted. "And I don't want to move to Pennsylvania!"

I've never seen Willa be bad before. She stamped her feet and the cards got all messed up.

"Uh-oh," Penny said. Mrs. Getter bent down to clean them up, and Mom told her not to worry about it.

I went to my desk to get the Play-Doh turtle. "Here," I told Willa. "You can have this to remember me by."

Willa took it from me and turned back to her mom. "What if—what if kids in Pennsylvania don't know how to play Spit?"

"Oh Willa," Mrs. Getter said. She opened up her arms and Willa fell into her. Mrs. Getter picked Willa up and carried her out of my room. Mom went with them, but I stayed where I was. I told Penny to go out of my room. I knew it wasn't a nice thing to say, but I really didn't want her to be with me right then.

I didn't know what to do about the cards. I didn't want to put them away because we were still in the middle of playing. But they were all messed up, so we wouldn't be able to finish our game anyway.

Mom came back in my room and I was afraid I was going to get in trouble for being mean to Penny. But she didn't say anything about Penny. She just said, "We're going to have to be extra sensitive to Willa for the next few weeks. This is very hard on her."

"It's hard on me too," I said. "You're not even sad that Willa is leaving!"

"Of course I'm sad," Mom said.

"No, you were just mad about my hair," I told her. "You hate it."

"I'm getting used to it," Mom said. "It looks cute, like a pixie cut."

"If you really thought it was cute you would let Penny cut her hair too. But you got mad and punished us because you didn't want Penny to look like me."

"I don't mind if Penny cuts her hair," Mom said. "If she wants short hair, that's fine.

But it wasn't okay for her to use her hair like a paintbrush. That's not what hair is for."

"Yesterday you said it was exciting that Willa was moving. Exciting means you think it's a good thing."

"I said that because Gayle—Mrs. Getter—told me Willa was really upset about the move," Mom said. "Before Willa was dropped

off yesterday, she'd been crying about it, and I didn't want to upset her all over again. You saw how she was just now."

"I think Willa was bad because of me," I said.

"What do you mean?"

"I made this pudding at Batts Confections. It had magical ingredients and I gave it to Willa so she wouldn't have to move away."

"You know that's just pretend," Mom said.

"But Penny made a finding-Belinda potion, and right after, you called to say you found her. Maybe my potion turned Willa bad, so her parents would have to stay here in Somers."

"Oh Stel," Mom said. "The truth is there's nothing you or Willa can do to stop this move."

I didn't say anything back to her.

Sometimes it's hard to think of the right words, even for people who want to be writers when they grow up.

"You know," Mom said, "there's a famous chocolate place in Pennsylvania that Daddy and I have always wanted to take you girls to. Maybe we can plan a trip and visit the Getters, too. I hear they're going to have a zip line in their backyard."

"What's a zip line?" I asked.

"It's a special wire that you set up between two trees," Mom said. "There's a seat attached, and you can ride on it from one tree to the next."

"Can we really visit Willa in Pennsylvania?" I asked.

"Of course," Mom said. "I want to try out the zip line."

"If you go on the zip line when you're

pregnant, it would probably be a fun ride for the baby," I said.

"I bet," Mom said. "But Willa's not moving for a month. Your brother will already be born by the time we visit."

"There's one thing I don't understand," I said.

"What's that?" Mom asked.

"How come all of Penny's wishes keep coming true, and none of mine do?"

"I don't know," Mom said. "Maybe because you're older—you're wishing for things that are harder to get. Penny was wishing for things that were going to happen anyway."

"I'm not trying to wish for hard things," I said.

"I have an idea," Mom said. "Why don't you make a wish list of all the things you want to do with Willa before she goes? Daddy and

I will do our best to make sure you and Willa get to do as many things on your wish list as possible. Okay?"

"Okay," I said.

"Good," Mom said.

"Mom, can I ask you a question?"

"You can ask me anything."

"Well, the thing is, I know the magic stuff was pretend. But is it okay I still believe in it? Like not completely, but sort of?"

"Of course, Stel," Mom said. "I still believe in magic, too. A long time ago, I wished I'd have a daughter exactly like you, and now here you are."

"You want me even with my ugly hair?"

"Your hair is not ugly," Mom said. "And I want you no matter what."

Then she gave me a hug. She asked if I wanted to help her with dinner, but I said no.

I wanted to get started on my wish list. Mom made spaghetti and meatballs, which is my favorite dinner in the whole entire world. I didn't even tell Mom I wanted it, but she knew and she made it for me. So that's sort of like having a wish that came true.

And then after school on Monday, which was the very next day, Mom took Willa and me to the first place on my list, which was the Somers Rec Center, where they have a giant trampoline. Willa and I had a jumping contest, doing these jumps that we saw on *Superstar Sam.* Well, sort of like Superstar Sam, because we couldn't do the flips. But we both jumped really high. Mom said she couldn't tell which one of us was higher, so it was a tie. It's fun to tie with your best friend.

That's it for now. That's the end of the story. Maybe I should write "the end."

THE END

P.S. It's not the end forever because I'm going to write another book one day. It's just the end of book two.

Stella's Wish List

1. Go on the trampoline at the Somers Rec Center and do a routine like Superstar Sam

2. Invent a special kind of fudge called "Best Friends" fudge to sell at Batts Confections

3. Go to the beach

4. Picnic at the redwood forest

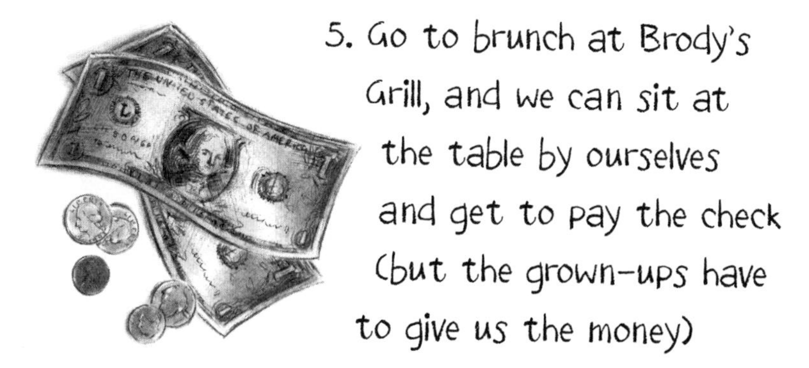

5. Go to brunch at Brody's Grill, and we can sit at the table by ourselves and get to pay the check (but the grown-ups have to give us the money)

6. Ride the roller coaster at Somerland Amusement Park (but not the really big one)

7. Have a sleepover at Willa's house and stay up really REALLY late

8. The biggest Spit tournament

Sneak preview of

Stella Batts

Pardon Me

Book

Carpool

Remember me? I'm Stella Batts. This is my third book. Maybe you've read my first two books. If you haven't, you can start right here.

My mom says if you write at least three books that are all connected then you have a series. So when this book is finished I'll be the author of a series! Hooray!

But so far I'm only on Chapter 1. Here's a list of things that happened since the end of my last book:

1. My best friend, Willa, moved away to Pennsylvania.
2. I changed my favorite color from yellow to blue.
3. My hair grew an eensy weensy bit so it isn't as short as a pixie cut anymore, but it's still not long enough for a ponytail. Sometimes I clip the sides up with barrettes.

Friday afternoons, it's Mom's turn to drive us home from school. "Us" means me, my little sister, Penny, and her best friend, Zoey. It used to mean Willa too, before she moved.

Today Dad's car pulled up in the school parking lot. Mom is pregnant, and her stomach has gotten super big. It's hard for her to squeeze into the driver's seat behind the steering wheel. So Dad has been doing carpool instead. That's another thing that changed since my last book.

After we were all buckled in, Dad started to drive away. "Okay, what game are we playing?" he asked. When Dad carpools, we play car games.

"Geography," I said.

This is how you play Geography. You think of the name of a place, like Arkansas. And then the next person has to use the last letter of your place, which would be an "s." So they could say something like Salt Lake City. The person after that would have to use the "y." It goes on and on until you can't think of any more places.

"I hate that game," Penny said. "Stella knows more places because she's eight, so it's not fair. How about I Spy?"

You probably already know the game I

Spy, but just in case, it's when you say, "I spy with my little eye," and then you describe something you see out the window. Like, "something green," or "something metal." The other players try to guess before we drive by and can't see it anymore.

"We ALWAYS play that game," I said.

"Zoey will be our deciding vote," Dad said.

Penny clasped her hands together and leaned toward Zoey. "Please, pretty please, pick I Spy," she said. "I'll be your best friend."

Zoey giggled. "You already are my best friend," she said. "Okay, it's I Spy."

If Willa were the deciding vote, it would have been Geography, but of course Zoey picked I Spy.

"Yay!" Penny said. "I'll go first. I spy with my little eye."

"What?" Zoey asked.

"Hold on, I'm still spying."

We drove past Lee Avenue, which is the street Willa used to live on. I knew she wouldn't be there, but I turned my head to look anyway.

"Dad, what time is it?" I asked.

"It's two-fifty," he said.

I had been trying to call Willa, but it's hard because of the time change. Pennsylvania is three hours later than California, which meant it was 5:50 there. That's a good time to call. "Can I use your cell phone please?"

"I'll get it for you at the next red light."

There was a traffic light up ahead, and it turned red just as we got to it. Dad handed me his phone.

"I spy with my little eye something yellow and red," Penny said.

Zoey started guessing as I dialed. I pressed the phone against my ear. Mrs. Getter answered after two rings.

"Hi, it's Stella Batts. Is Willa there?"

"Stella Batts, how lovely to hear your voice. She's just in the other room. Hold on a moment." I heard her put the phone down, and then I heard her call out, "Willa! Stella's on the phone!"

And then I heard Willa say, "I don't want to talk to her."

Those are exactly the words I heard: I don't want to talk to her.

But I knew I must have heard her wrong. Why wouldn't Willa want to talk to me? I didn't do anything wrong.

Or did I? I thought about the things we did before Willa left Somers. We played a hundred games of Spit, we had a bunch of sleepovers, we went to Brody's Grill and sat by ourselves at the table. We never fought. She was never mad at me, not once!

Mrs. Getter picked up the phone again. "I'm sorry, Stel. We're headed out for a picnic dinner, but I'll make sure she calls you back another time."

A picnic with Willa in the redwood forest had been number 4 on my wish list of things to do before Willa moved away, but we didn't have time to go. Now she was going without me—not to the redwood forest, but somewhere in Pennsylvania. Maybe somewhere she liked even better. And she wouldn't even talk to me first. That seemed kind of mean. I didn't understand. Willa is NEVER a meanie.

Is it possible that she moved to Pennsylvania and turned mean? Oh no, I hoped not.

Mrs. Getter said goodbye. I heard the phone click when she hung up. I kept the phone pressed to my ear for a few more seconds, just waiting. Maybe Willa would come to the phone after all. But I knew the line was dead and she really wouldn't.

Courtney Sheinmel

Courtney Sheinmel is the author of several books for middle-grade readers, including *Sincerely* and *All The Things You Are*. Like Stella Batts, she was born in California and has a younger sister. However, her parents never owned a candy store. Now Courtney lives in New York City, where she has tasted all the cupcakes in her neighborhood. She also makes a delicious cookie brownie graham-cracker pie. Visit her at www.courtneysheinmel.com, where you can find the recipe along with information about the Stella Batts books.

Jennifer A. Bell

Jennifer A. Bell is a children's book illustrator whose work can also be found in magazines, on greeting cards, and on the occasional Christmas ornament. She studied Fine Arts at the Columbus College of Art and Design and currently lives in Minneapolis, Minnesota.

In this early chapter book series, the ups and downs of Stella's life are charmingly chronicled. She's in third grade, she wants to be a writer, and her parents own a candy shop. Life should be sweet, right?

Read more about Stella in

Stella Batts

Pardon Me

J Fic SHE
Sheinmel, Courtney.
Stella Batts :
Book 2 : Stella Batts hair
R15